11-17.18

Board to
Death
Amanda Blakemore
Mystery Book 2

By
Amy Phipps

Editing by Ebookeditingpro

Dedication

To God who has been so good to me in my life.

Special thanks to my mother for reading all my books before they are completed.

And to my loving husband Matthew

Chapter 1

Amanda Blakemore tugged the suitcase out of the back of her late grandfather's 1994 Lincoln Town Car. She swiped at the long blonde strands of hair blowing in her face before closing the trunk. Turning around to face her grandmother's Victorian home, now her home, too, a smile spread across her face. She marveled at how much her life had changed in just a short span of time. Since she moved back to Juniper Falls, Ohio, to live with her grandmother, things had been interesting; a cheating husband, eccentric new friends, a couple of new jobs, and a murder. Strange thing about it, though, was that she was happier than she had ever been.

Balancing the suitcase and a cup of coffee in one hand, she turned the knob on the front door and pushed it open. "I'm home!" she called. Gently setting down everything on the bench beside the door, she could hear loud clicking noises racing toward her from the living room. She braced herself for what was coming. Twinkie, a giant St. Bernard, slammed into her, nearly toppling her over.

"Twinkie," Amanda exclaimed, laughing as she bent down to hug him and ruffle his ears. "I see someone missed me," she said with a grin. "You know I was only gone two days."

"Two days is a long time to a dog," announced

Margaret, Amanda's grandmother, who was making her way in from the kitchen. Margaret carried a tray with a bowl of potato chips, glasses, and cans of pop. "Come into the living room, Olive is here," she said.

Olive Simpson was her grandmother's best friend and a little eccentric, to say the least, but Amanda had come to enjoy hanging out with the two women. Amanda kicked off her shoes to get more comfortable and plopped down on the couch.

"You're just in time. We're going to watch the next episode of Mulberry Lane," Olive announced, blinking her eyes like a large owl from behind her purple-framed glasses. "But it can wait. Your last two days probably had more drama than any soap opera." Olive leaned forward to get all the dirty details.

"Olive!" Margaret scolded, as she also leaned forward, waiting for information.

"Nothing happened really. We both showed up at the courthouse and then the divorce was finalized." Amanda shrugged and poured some cola into a glass of ice.

"That's it?" Margaret had a look of surprise across her aged, but beautiful, features.

"That's it. I'm officially divorced," Amanda answered, taking a drink from her glass.

"Did you at least get to tell off that floozy? She did steal your husband," Olive said, sounding somewhat disappointed.

"She didn't steal him ... he went willingly," Amanda pointed out. "Besides, she can have him." She gave a wave of her hand.

"Good riddance to bad rubbish." Margaret nodded her head, emphasizing every word.

"Your grandmother is right. You'll be all right. After all, you have us." Olive patted Amanda on the shoulder in a sympathetic manner.

"I'm not sad … I was at first. Now I'm just relieved that it's all over and I can continue on with my life," Amanda stated.

"That's the spirit," Olive cackled. "There's plenty more fish in the sea."

"I'm not really looking for anyone right now."

"That's good," Margaret announced, "because you're not going to have much time for romance with what I have planned for us."

"What's going on in that head of yours? Should I be worried?" Amanda asked with a concerned tone in her voice.

Margaret reached over the side of the chair arm and grabbed some papers from the end table, pushing them toward Amanda.

Looking down at the papers, Amanda read aloud, "Garden Competition? But we don't have a garden." She had a confused look on her face.

"We have the backyard and it needs a lot of work but I think we can do it. Also, the winner gets two thousand dollars."

"That's a lot of money," Amanda said, a little impressed by the amount.

"I want to give it to the church for their building fund for the new roof," Margaret announced proudly.

"And I want your grandmother to win so she

can stick it to my neighbor, Mr. Peabody. He wins every year and is a very sore winner," Olive snorted in disgust.

"Olive, that's not why I'm doing this," Margaret scolded, rolling her eyes at her friend.

"I know that ... it's just, that would be an added bonus," Olive said, with a sweet old lady smile of pure innocence. "Also, we would get to host the garden party. The winner always gets to be the host of the garden party." She grinned sheepishly. Olive thought she had perfected the sweet old lady act, but Amanda knew better.

Giggling at Olive, she interrupted, saying, "I think that's a wonderful idea but I don't know anything about gardening."

"Well, I've been using the internet and have

plenty of ideas, and we can ask Henry to help us. He does all his own gardening," Margaret informed the others.

Henry was their next door neighbor and the ex-sheriff of Juniper Falls. He and Amanda had become good friends since he helped save her life.

"Then count me in," Amanda agreed.

≈

Amanda was busying herself wiping the counter of the small diner where she worked part time in the evenings. She needed to work another job because her dog-sitting job didn't pay her bills. The smell of fresh apple pie was wafting from the kitchen. Deb, the diner's owner, made the best apple pie in the whole of Juniper Falls and everyone knew it.

"Did you at least buy yourself something nice while you were in Chicago?" the rotund woman called, as she looked up from the oven.

"I would have to have money to do that." Amanda laughed, grabbing a plate from the window and delivered it to a customer who was sitting quietly at table five.

"If its money you're wanting, you're working in the wrong place," joked Wendy, the curvy red-haired waitress, as she cleared the dirty dishes from a recently vacated table.

"Money isn't everything," Deb announced, shaking her spatula in the air.

"It makes people do horrible things," Amanda said quietly. Stopping at table four, she smiled. "Hello, Jacob, what can I get for you today?"

Jacob Marsdale had become a regular at the diner over the past few months. He always sat at the same table and ordered the same thing, but first Jacob would make a big production of trying to decide what to order. Amanda got the impression he was a bit lonely.

Jacob's wife was away visiting her sister out of state. Amanda studied the top of his head, waiting patiently for him to respond. Jacob was an older gentleman but not as old as his hair style of choice would make him. He wore it longer on one side and combed the mousey brown strands over to the other side to hide his bald patch.

Looking up from his menu, he used his index finger to push his wire-rimmed glasses up his pointy nose. "I'll have the fried chicken dinner and some sweet tea."

"You want your usual apple pie for dessert?" Amanda asked, tapping her pen on her order pad.

"You're a mind reader." Jacob handed her his menu and smiled pleasantly.

Amanda started to walk away, but then she turned back around and said, "I've been meaning to ask you. Do you have an application for the garden competition? Nana plans to enter this year."

"Of course I do. I'm the president of the garden club." He beamed with pride. "How about I drop one off later this week?"

"That would be great."

The bell above the door rang and Butch Henderson came strutting in and slapped Wendy on the behind. "Hello, beautiful," he crowed, taking a seat at the counter. "We still on for tonight?"

Wendy smiled and giggled. "Absolutely, as long as you behave."

Amanda was cutting a piece of apple pie and placing it on a plate when the bell jingled again. "Hey, Jonah," she called, making her way over to Jacob and placing the plate of pie down in front of him. "Give me a second and I'll get your take-out order," she added.

"Still working on it!" Deb exclaimed from the window.

"I'm not in a hurry, take your time," Jonah said, taking a seat at the counter. Jonah was the local doctor and owner of Twinkie, the St. Bernard that Amanda walked.

"Did you get my text?" Amanda asked. "You

can pick up Twinkie at Nana's. I took him for a long walk down by the Falls and it wore him out pretty good."

"Maybe he won't bark all night." Jonah laughed, running his hand through his hair. He was making a joke about how they met.

"We can only hope," Amanda whispered quietly, leaning in across the counter, laughter shinning in her big blue eyes. "I would hate to have to come and bang on your door at midnight again."

"I hate to interrupt, Doc, but I need to pay for this," Butch said, holding up his coffee for Jonah to see and flashing Amanda a charming smile and a wink of his brown eyes.

"I didn't know you were back in town, Butch," Jonah commented.

"Been back about a month," he answered, scratching his stubbly chin.

"Keeping yourself out of trouble?" Jonah asked doubtfully.

"Yeah, got my own lawn business." Butch puffed his chest out with pride. "It keeps me busy."

"Not too busy, I hope." Wendy said in a flirty tone and giggled.

"Never too busy for you, babe," Butch flirted back, as he made his way to the door. "If you need some help with your lawn Doc, give me a call."

Deb came trotting out from the kitchen with a paper bag and set it on the counter. "That man is a hopeless flirt. You should stay away from that one," she called to Wendy.

"I'm not looking to get married, just to have a

little fun." Wendy shrugged one of her thin shoulders.

"That girl!" Deb tossed her hands in the air. "Your order, Doc." She pointed to the bag on the counter.

"Thanks, Deb." He turned to leave, then stopped and turned back around. "Amanda, can I drop off Twinkie a little later tomorrow?"

"Sure thing. If there's no answer at the front door, come around back." At his look of confusion, she continued, "Nana has me working on the garden tomorrow."

"I guess your weekend is all planned out for you, then." He laughed.

"With what she wants done, probably most of my summer." She laughed and waved goodbye to him as he backed out the door.

≈

It was late the next morning when Jonah

knocked on the front door of the Victorian. Getting

know answer, he made his way around the side of

the house. Twinkie sniffed the bushes along the way.

Jonah could hear voices drifting from the backyard.

As he rounded the corner, he could see Amanda

swiping a stray strand of blonde hair from her face

with her gloved hand. She succeeded in smudging

dirt down her lightly freckled cheek as she took a

shovel and edged the flowerbed.

A smile spread across his face at the thought

of their first meeting. Amanda had yelled at him in

the middle of the night about his barking dog. He's

never been treated like that by a woman before. She intrigued him. It didn't hurt that she was gorgeous and she seemed to have absolutely no clue of her effect on the opposite sex. He was certain that she had no idea that he was interested in her, but timing was everything in these in these matters. Now was not the time, he kept telling himself. He wanted to give her time to get over her divorce.

Twinkie finally noticed Amanda and in his excitement, he bolted as fast and as hard as he could and slammed into her, knocking her over. Then he started licking her face. "You Stupid Dog," she yelled. "Stop slobbering on me." She shoved at the massive creature but to no avail.

"Guess I should save you." Jonah laughed, grabbing Twinkie's collar and pulling him off of her.

"My hero," she announced with sarcasm, wiping her face on her pink shirt. "A true hero would have saved me before I ended up on the ground." Amanda gave him a dirty look as she climbed to her feet and dusted off her jean shorts.

"I'll work on my timing." He grinned, trying to stifle a laugh.

"Good morning, Dr. Winters," Margaret called. She made her way over to where he was standing, with Olive close to her heels.

"Good morning, Mrs. Blakemore." He nodded his head. "Mrs. Simpson."

"You're here to drop off Twinkie?" Olive asked, smiling from under the brim of her large sun hat. Her glasses made her eyes look three times larger than normal as she batted them at Jonah.

Hopeless flirt, Amanda thought, as she tried to stifle a laugh at the embarrassed expression on his face at Olive's obvious advances.

"I am," he answered, his face bright pink.

Margaret interrupted, "I'm glad you're here. I was wondering if you would mind if I paint the fence that separates our backyards."

"It does look bad where I had to patch it, because someone busted a large hole in it," he said, looking at Twinkie, who snorted at the mention of his misdeeds and then continued digging a hole.

"He looks very remorseful." Amanda laughed.

"I'm going to enter my backyard in the garden competition this year and I want to win," Margaret admitted.

"I'm taking some vacation time from work

and I need a project so I can paint the fence for you," he offered. "Maybe I can make up for Twinkie's barking at night?"

"I don't want you to feel obligated," Margaret said, unsure.

"Don't look a gift horse in the mouth." Olive nudged Margaret in the side. "If the man wants to do it then let him."

"I'm with Olive," Amanda chimed in. "We're going to need all the help we can get to win that prize money for the church."

"You're planning on giving the winnings to the church?" Jonah asked with a surprised tone in his voice.

"For the building fund to replace the roof," Olive said.

"That's very thoughtful," Jonah said. "How about I start tomorrow morning on the fence."

"Sounds good." Margaret's face beamed with excitement.

"So it's a date, then," Jonah said, returning her smile. He glanced at his watch. "I better get to work."

The three women watched as he turned and walked away, rubbing Twinkie's head before completely disappearing out of sight.

"Well, at least we'll have something nice to look at while we're doing all this manual labor," Olive cackled, slapping Amanda on the back.

"Olive, you are terrible," Amanda announced, laughing and shaking her head.

Chapter 2

The next morning, Amanda awoke to gentle taps on her forehead. Moaning, she rolled over in her bed. Her eyes were still closed and she could feel more gentle taps on her temple. Releasing a long sigh, she groaned, "Ghost ... Really." She slowly opened her eyes to see the fuzzy gray cat with large green eyes sitting on her pillow.

"Meow," he purred and tapped her again.

"You're not going to stop until I get up, are you?" She reached out and scratched him under his chin and he purred louder. "You do realize that its 6 o'clock in the morning and this is the only day I could have slept in." Tossing the covers to the side, she moaned again. All that edging around the flowerbeds from the day before had taken a toll on her muscles. Standing, she stretched and shoved her feet into her slippers, then walked downstairs with Ghost hot on her heels.

In the kitchen, she retrieved a can of tuna from the cabinet, and started opening the can as Ghost twirled himself around her ankles as if saying, "Thank you, I love you." She set the plate on the floor and stroked his gray fur a couple of times.

Hearing footsteps behind her, Amanda stood and turned to see her Nana standing in the doorway. Margaret was fully dressed in a pair of blue jeans and a T-shirt with little roses sprinkled all over it. Her silver hair was piled in a bun and she plopped a large-brimmed hat on her head to keep the sun off her face.

"Wow ... You're already dressed," Amanda said, surprised. "I can barely move."

"I'm so excited ... I have the whole garden planned out and when it's finished it'll be beautiful." Margaret smiled, grabbing some oats from the pantry and a pan from the cabinet. "You need to get dressed. Olive and Henry will be here soon."

"When you mentioned an early start I didn't think you meant this early," Amanda protested.

"The heat and old people don't mix well, so I want to get out there and get as much done before it gets too hot. After all, it is June," Margaret explained, heating up a pan of water on the stove.

"Say no more," Amanda held her hand up in a gesture of surrender. "I'll get dressed."

"I can make you some oats for breakfast," Margaret offered.

"You're the best, Nana, and maybe some coffee." Amanda smiled, her blue eyes pleading.

"You are spoiled, young lady." Margaret laughed, watching her granddaughter exit the kitchen. Then Margaret looked down at Ghost, who was rubbing on her legs, and she scolded, "That, sir, is your second can of tuna this morning. Don't think I didn't notice."

≈

Amanda was fighting to dig up a dead shrub when she heard a male voice say, "Hey, freckles, need some help?" She turned to see Henry Walters standing there in bib-overalls with a glass of ice water in his hand, which he reached out to offer her.

"Henry! I would love some help." She beamed, swiping at her forehead with a gloved hand before taking the glass from him and taking a long drink. "I haven't seen you for days."

"I went to visit my nephew in Columbus for a few days," Henry informed her, taking the shovel from her hand to give her a break.

"I hope you had a good rest because Nana is a slave driver." She laughed, glancing over at Nana.

"Compared to spending three days with my nephew and his three kids, this will be a breeze," Henry said, pointing at the dead shrub.

"Hey, guys,'" Jonah called from the gate,

drawing their attention. Twinkie was following close behind him. "Reporting for duty, Ms. Margaret." Flashing her a bright smile before releasing Twinkie from his leash, he continued, "I didn't know what color to get for the fence so I thought I would ask you and then go pick it up at the hardware store."

"I'll write it down for you," Margaret said, picking up a pen and paper from the work table. "Can Amanda go with you? I need her to pick up a few things, too."

"Sure, if she wants to," he answered.

"Amanda," Margaret called. "Would you go to the hardware store with Dr. Winters and pick up some stuff for me?"

Amanda walked over to her grandmother and pulled off her gloves. "Sure," she said, holding out her hand for the list. "Oh, don't let him overdo it," she whispered and motioned with her thumb toward Henry.

"I won't," Margaret whispered back and winked at her granddaughter.

≈

Amanda winced as she climbed into Jonah's black pickup truck. Her muscles weren't accustomed to all the gardening that she had performed over the last two days. "You don't know what you're getting yourself into," she announced, as she put on her seat belt. Amanda glanced at Jonah. He sure did look handsome in his blue jeans and tight-fitting red T-shirt.

She had never noticed how muscular he was until now. All she had ever seen him in was dress pants with button up shirts and ties. Well, except for the very first time they had met. Then, he had been in pajama pants and a baggy T-shirt. His hair wasn't perfectly styled today, either, she noted. Amanda liked the way his dark blonde hair was a little messy. It made him seem less intimidating.

His deep voice interrupted her thoughts. "Sore muscles?"

It took her mind a few minutes to understand what he was referring to before she responded. "Muscles I didn't even know I had are killing me."

"They'll start to feel better in a couple of days," Jonah admitted. "It's just torture until then."

"Is that your professional opinion, Doc?" she asked sarcastically.

"Yeah it is." He said as he slowed his truck

down to enter the parking lot of the hardware store. Climbing out wasn't nearly as bad as climbing in, she realized, as she made her way around the truck to where Jonah was waiting for her so they could enter the store together.

"That wasn't as bad as I thought it would be," she commented, rubbing the top of her thigh.

Before he could respond, loud angry voices drew their attention. From what Amanda could see, the voices belonged to Butch Henderson and Marty Smith. She knew both of them from the diner. Marty owned a lawn care business.

"You think I don't know what you're up to," Marty yelled, pointing his finger in Butch's face.

"Its business, dude." Butch shrugged his shoulders.

"I'm not going to stand by and let you steal all my business," Marty roared, shaking his fist in the air.

"And who's going to stop me?" Butch sneered, and with a chuckle continued, "You?"

Before Marty could say any more, Michael Simpson came up to the arguing men and said calmly, "Fellas, you're scaring away my customers. If you don't want me to call Sheriff Thomas, you need to leave." Michael was twice the size of the other two men and the threat of the Sheriff was effective.

Both men glared at each other. "This isn't over," Marty hissed, before getting into his truck and leaving. Butch did the same, squealing rubber on the way out of the parking lot.

Michael turned to go back into the store and

simply said, "Some people have absolutely no sense."

He held the door for Amanda and Jonah.

Chapter 3

It was hot and Amanda poured sweat as she fought with yet another shrub that Margaret swore had to go for the garden to be perfect. She heaved a deep sigh and swiped at a bead of perspiration running down her forehead before tossing her shovel to the ground.

"It's not that bad, is it?" Jonah laughed, fighting with his own shrub.

"This thing won't budge, maybe I should go

help Henry with the gate." Amanda motioned toward Henry, who was replacing the old metal gate with a new one.

"It will just be waiting for you when you get back." Jonah grunted as he pulled his shrub free. "Triumph!" He smiled brightly, tossing the old shrub off to the side.

Amanda gave him a dirty look. "Don't rub it in." She growled and picked up her shovel to continue the fight.

Reaching down, he grabbed a bottle of water and took a long drink. "I'll make you a deal," he offered.

She stopped working to look into his brown eyes. "I'm listening."

"If you help me stain the fence, I'll finish

digging up that shrub." He pointed to the poor abused shrub.

"You have a deal!" She grinned as she extended her hand and they shook on it. She took a few steps back to give him room to work and plopped down on the grass. "Are you sure this is how you want to spend your vacation?" she asked.

He shrugged, leaning on his shovel. "I don't mind. I love being outside. As a doctor, I don't get to spend a lot of time outdoors."

"Woof! Woof!" Twinkie started barking, jumping up for his shady spot under the maple tree.

"What's he barking at?" Amanda asked, turning to see Butch Henderson strolling into the backyard.

"Hello," Butch called to everyone with a wave

of the hand.

Margaret and Olive looked up from their discussion of what color the flowers should be. Olive wanted purple, of course, while Margaret wanted a mixture. Margaret smiled and walked over to greet Butch. "Hello, how have you been?"

"Great, just great," he said, shaking Margaret's hand.

Olive followed close behind. "Hello, Butch, I thought you moved away," she said, batting her eyes from behind her large, purple-framed glasses and smoothing her hair.

"I did for about two years but there's no place like home." He gave her a charming smile. "Wendy said you were doing work for the garden competition. I thought maybe I could give you a bid."

"Amanda said you started a landscaping business. We're going to do all the planting ourselves but ..." Margaret motioned for him to follow her over to the table where she had her plans. "I want to put a stone patio here." She pointed at the paper. "So, if you want to give me a bid for that."

Olive chimed in a flirtatious voice. "Yeah, a big strong man like yourself."

Henry walked over to where Jonah and Amanda were standing and whispered, "That woman is man crazy."

Amanda giggled. "I think it gives her character."

"You only say that because she's not chasing after you," Henry said, wagging his finger at her.

"Hello, Amanda," Jacob Marsdale called. He

drew everyone's attention to himself as he made his way across the yard. "I have your application for the garden competition," he said.

"Thanks," she said, taking the papers from him.

"Henry, Dr. Winters, how's life been treating you?" Jacob asked with a nod of his head.

"Good. Margaret's been working us all pretty hard." Henry laughed. "She's pretty excited about this project."

Looking around the garden, Jacob said, "Looks good! She just might win this year."

"That's the plan." Amanda smiled. "Let me get Nana for you."

"That's okay, she looks busy. I just wanted to drop off her paperwork. Make sure she turns it in before the deadline or she won't be able to even enter the competition."

"Will do," Amanda said, giving him a mock salute.

"Keep up the good work," Jacob called, as he made his way toward the gate.

"Jacob," Margaret called and waved him over to where she and Butch were standing. "How lovely to see you Amanda told me you would be stopping by."

Butch ignored the older man's presence and announced. "I'll pick up those stones you ordered and drop them off tonight." Butch rubbed his hands together, "I have to mow a couple of lawns. Then, I can get started on your patio."

"That will be fine," Margaret continued. "If

I'm not here, go ahead and let yourself into the backyard. I've got church tonight."

"I'll see you tomorrow," he said.

"Mrs. Blakemore." Jacob said, "Your garden is looking lovely and you have lots of help. Just wanted to let you know that I brought your application for the competition." He motioned toward the papers in Amanda's hand. "I best get going. You're not the only application I need to drop off today."

"Thanks so much for dropping it by." Margaret waved as he made his way through the gate.

≈

That evening, Amanda sat filling salt shakers at the diner. It was after the dinner rush and she was glad to rest her tired feet. Wendy busied herself washing the tables as Deb spent her time cutting up apples for one of her famous pies. The bell above the door jingled and a raven-haired woman came prancing in, wearing hot pink high heels and a black spandex dress that showed way too much skin. Amanda hopped off her stool and smiled politely. "What can I get for you?"

"You can stay away from my boyfriend," the woman demanded.

"Excuse me?" Amanda's blue eyes grew to the size of saucers.

"Butch is mine, and I don't like to share," the woman screamed, pointing her finger in Amanda's face.

"You're picking a fight with the wrong girl. Butch has been seeing me," Wendy interrupted, tossing down her dishtowel on the table and walking

over to the woman. "Who are you?"

"Lydia Benson ... Butch's girlfriend." Her

voice dripped with sarcasm as she bobbed her head.

"Funny, he's never mentioned having a

girlfriend." Wendy gave Lydia a pitying smile.

"Maybe you're overstating your worth."

Lydia's red lips opened and closed like a fish

from the insult. "Just stay away from MY MAN!" She

pointed her finger in Wendy's face before turning on

her high heels and storming out of the diner.

Amanda put her hand on Wendy's shoulder

and said, "I'm sorry."

"I'm going to find that no good cheating ..."

Wendy jerked off her apron and tossed it on the

counter with tears in her eyes. "Slime-ball!"

Deb came out of the kitchen and said, "Don't you worry about us, we can hold down the fort."

Deb and Amanda watched as Wendy marched out the door. "I knew that man was bad news." Deb sighed, shaking her head. "Too flirty." She wrinkled her nose in disgust.

"I hope she's going to be all right," Amanda worried, watching from the window as Wendy's car pulled out of the parking lot.

≈

It was late when Amanda walked up the steps of the porch to see Ghost sitting patiently by the front door, tapping his bushy gray tail. The street light made his yellow eyes glow. "Good evening, been waiting long?" she asked, reaching down and rubbing his head. He purred and danced around her legs as she pulled her keys out of her pocket and unlocked the door. Inside, she tossed her purse and keys on the side table as she called, "Nana, you home?"

"In the kitchen," Margaret answered. Ghost ran ahead of her into the kitchen.

"You been home long?" Amanda asked, noticing her grandmother still wearing her church clothes.

"No, just got home," she answered, not looking up from the papers she was reading.

Looking over Margaret's shoulder, Amanda asked, "Is that the entry form for the garden competition?"

"Yes, I've been reading all the rules and trying to fill it out perfectly so the judges accept our application." Margaret finally glanced up from her work. "Look out back and see if Butch delivered the patio stones and mulch."

Standing on her tiptoes, Amanda peeked out the kitchen window. She could see a large shadow that looked like the patio stones and bags of mulch. "Looks like it, from what I can see." Turning around and grabbing a can of soda from the fridge and some dry cat food from the pantry, she filled Ghost's bowl. Plopping down at the table, she opened her soda and took a long drink. "I'm exhausted."

"Finished!" Margaret declared, putting down her pencil and turning her full attention to her granddaughter. "How was work?"

"Drama," was the only answer Amanda gave to her grandmother's question.

Margaret perked up, raising her eyebrows. "Really?"

"Long story." Amanda waved her hand and sighed. "Mind if I tell you about it tomorrow? I just want to sleep."

"It's late. I think it's time for all of us to get to bed." Margaret got up from the table and wagged her finger at Amanda. "Just don't forget to tell me."

Amanda laughed, turning off the light as she followed her grandmother out of the room. "Don't worry. If I forget to tell you, I'm sure Olive will have heard all about it by then and she'll tell you."

Chapter 4

Amanda awoke the next morning to sore muscles, moving her feet slowly under the blankets to test her limbs. She gently stretched. Ghost perched himself at the foot of the bed. He noticed the blankets moving, so he made his move, jumping on her feet and wrapping his front paws around her legs, kicking her with his back paws. "Ghost!" She laughed and launched a counter attack and wrapped him up in the blankets with her feet. "Gotcha!"

Crawling to the foot of the bed, she uncovered the cat and tussled the gray fur on the top of his head. "Meow," he complained.

"You can have the bed. I've got to shower," she said, jumping out of bed.

The shower soothed her muscles so much that she hated to get out. But she had a long day ahead of her, she told herself. Amanda forced herself to get out of the shower and get dressed before going downstairs to the kitchen.

Grabbing a cup out of the cabinet, she poured herself some coffee. "Good morning, Nana."

Margaret was flipping through a flower magazine. "What do you think of these?" She pointed to a picture of some purple impatiens.

"Those are beautiful, and Olive would be

happy," Amanda said with a laugh, as she leaned against the counter and sipped her coffee.

Ghost tangled himself around her ankles and then scratched at the back door. Amanda opened the door and let the large tomcat out into the backyard. Stepping out onto the back porch, she could feel the morning sun on her face and the cool dew on her bare feet.

Taking another sip from her coffee mug, she watched as Ghost made his way across the porch bannister and jumped onto the stack of patio stones that Butch had delivered last night. Ghost crouched down from his perch atop the stones then launched himself into the air, landing on a pair of brown work boots.

A chill ran down Amanda's spine as she

gently set her coffee mug on the bannister and climbed down the stairs. Her feet were wet and cold from the grass as she walked around the edge of the paving stones. Her blue eyes widened as the image of the lifeless body of Butch came into focus. His eyes were wide open, fixed, staring at the sky. Blood was everywhere. Someone had smashed in his skull. There was no doubt he was dead and had been for some time.

Amanda covered her mouth with her hand as she stared at the body in shock. Ghost chose that moment to grab her ankle making her scream. She jumped backwards and lost her balance, falling to the ground hard. Margaret yelled from the kitchen door, "Amanda, are you all right?"

Amanda tried to catch her breath and will her

heart to stop beating out of her chest as she climbed to her feet. "Butch Henderson is dead!"

"WHAT!" Margaret rushed out the kitchen door and down the steps. She gasped at the sight of the body. Placing her hand over her chest, she said, "You better call the Sheriff. I'll stay with the body."

"Yeah ... I'll call the sheriff." Giving herself a mental shake, Amanda placed her hand on Margaret's shoulder. "You going to be all right for a few minutes?"

"I'll be fine," Margaret reassured her with a squeeze of the hand.

Amanda reached down and picked up Ghost and said, "You're coming with me."

"Meow," the large gray tomcat complained.

≈

It didn't take Sheriff Thomas long to get there and drape the entire backyard with yellow police tape. Amanda watched from the porch as Margaret gave a statement to the deputy, with Henry by her side for moral support. Amanda had called Henry right after she called the sheriff. She had a feeling of overwhelming dread filling up her insides. This murder was far too close for comfort. What is going on here, she asked herself.

Glancing back to where the body lay, she saw Jonah examining the remains before they carted it off. Jonah climbed the stairs and looked at Amanda, a concerned expression on his handsome features. "You all right?"

"Yeah, this isn't my first dead body." She gave

him a weak smile. "Do you need to bring Twinkie over?" Jonah gave her a strange look. "Looks like your vacation is over," she added, nodding her head in the direction of the body.

"I suppose you're right. Do you mind?" he asked quietly.

"No, it will give me something to keep my mind off all this," she said, waving her hand toward the body.

"Here are my keys." He handed her the heavy metal ring. "You can get Twinkie when you're ready."

"What do you think killed him?" she asked, watching them lift Butch's body and place it on the gurney.

"Blow to the head with something heavy,"

Jonah said in a very matter-of-fact tone.

"I thought so," she said.

"Are you sure you're all right?" He gave her a concerned look.

"It's just … That could have been Nana or me." She pointed to where the body had been. "Sheriff Thomas thinks this was a botched robbery attempt … And Butch was at the wrong place at the wrong time." She looked at Jonah for reassurance.

"I don't think so," Jonah whispered so that the deputies couldn't hear him. "Butch still had his wallet and watch. If this was a robbery gone bad, they would have at least taken his wallet. It was full of cash."

"That doesn't make me feel better," she admitted.

"Did you hear anything?" he asked, putting his arm around her shoulders.

"No." She shook her head. "What time do you think?"

"Judging by the state of the body, between 7:30 and 9:30 last night." He sighed, running his hand through his hair.

"Nana was at church and I was at the diner until 9:30," Amanda informed. "Did you hear anything from your house?"

"No, I got home about 7:00 last night and took a shower, then fell asleep on the couch watching T.V. I didn't wake up until about midnight and then went to bed. Even Twinkie was quiet last night."

"He was probably tired from being outside most of the day. He's not used to it," Amanda suggested.

"What about Henry?" Jonah questioned.

"No, he was at church with Nana." Amanda shook her head.

"Didn't think so," he said, giving her hand a squeeze. "I'll stop by later and check on you girls when I pick up Twinkie."

"Thanks." She waved, watching him walk away. Turning, she looked at the empty ground again. Margaret's voice drew Amanda's attention. "They're finished with me. How about we go inside and get some coffee."

"Sounds good." Amanda forced a smile. "Henry, do you want some?"

"Yeah, I bought some muffins this morning." He shrugged. "That was before I realized you had a dead body in the backyard."

Olive came rushing out the back door and huffed. "What's going on? You have more traffic on your street than I've seen at the county fair."

"Someone murdered Butch Henderson last night. Amanda found the body this morning," Margaret answered, grabbing Olive by the shoulder and pushing her back though the kitchen door.

"That figures. The one time I sleep in, something interesting happens," Olive complained, tossing her hands into the air.

"Olive! This is not T.V. somebody's dead," Margaret scolded.

"Well, I know that!" Olive sat down at the table, looking rather put out.

"They haven't even got hold of the next of kin,

yet," Henry chimed in.

"Oh, no." Amanda grabbed Margaret's arm. "Wendy. I have to tell her before someone else does."

"What?" Margaret questioned, looking rather confused.

"Tell you on the way. Henry, can you handle this?" Amanda asked, tossing her thumb back toward the backyard.

"Sure." Henry shook his head.

"I've got to get Twinkie and then we'll be on our way." Amanda rushed out of the house.

"I'm going, too! I've already missed way too much, I'm not about to miss this," Olive announced, hot on Amanda's heels. "I can drive."

"No!" Margaret and Amanda announced in

unison.

Chapter 5

As Amanda tapped on Wendy's door, she could hear muffled crying from inside Twinkie danced nervously by her side. When the door opened, Wendy's wide green eyes were rimmed red from crying. Her red hair was a mess and she was still wearing her pajamas.

"You already heard," Amanda sighed she should have known news traveled fast in Juniper Falls. Amanda pulled Wendy in for a hug.

"Deb just left." She hiccupped. "She had to get back to the diner."

"I'm so sorry," Amanda said, squeezing her a little harder.

"Come on in." Wendy sniffed and opened the door wider to let them inside.

"Do you want me to make some tea?" Margaret offered.

Wendy gave her a weak smile. "It's in the cabinet next to the sink."

"Come on, Olive." Margaret grabbed Olive by the arm and practically dragged her to the kitchen.

Amanda and Wendy sat down on the couch as Twinkie roamed around the room, sniffing everything in sight.

"I know, I joked around about just having fun,

but I really cared for Butch," Wendy cried, burying her face in her hands. "Who would do something like this?"

"I don't know," Amanda answered, her voice filled with compassion as she rubbed Wendy's back. "Maybe it was that woman, the one from the diner. What was her name?"

"Lydia Benson," Wendy answered, raising her head and swiping at the tears in her eyes. "Just because your boyfriend is cheating on you doesn't give you a reason to kill him."

"It might for some people," Amanda added. "Did you get to talk to Butch after you left the diner last night?"

"No." Wendy blew her nose. "I started to look for him, you know, to confront him, but I decided I didn't want him to think I was too clingy so I came back here and ate a gallon of Rocky Road ice cream instead."

"Do you know of anyone else who didn't like Butch?"

"He complained about Ginger Meadows," Wendy answered, her voice a little hoarse from crying.

"I don't think I know her," Amanda admitted. "Why?"

Wendy looked a little embarrassed about her answer. "She claims her little boy belongs to Butch. She's always badgering him about child support."

"He doesn't claim the boy?" Amanda voiced her surprise.

"No, but the kid looks just like him," Wendy

informed her, heaving a deep sigh. "I know Butch wasn't the nicest guy, but ..." Her words trailed off, as she shrugged one shoulder.

"You were in love with him," Amanda supplied. Wendy merely shook her head in agreement.

Twinkie made his way over to Wendy and laid his head on her lap and whined. She smiled and rubbed his head. "He's trying to make you feel better." Amanda laughed.

≈

By the expression on Henry's face, he was glad to see the girls when they walked through the front door an hour later. "The sheriff left about half hour ago," he blurted out. "I was beginning to think he would never leave."

"Good!" Margaret exclaimed. "This has been the worst day. Ever!"

"I think I would have to agree," Amanda said, unhooking Twinkie's leash.

"Where's Olive?" Henry asked.

"She went to play cards—and gossip, too, if I know Olive," Margaret answered, waving her hand dismissively in the air. "Is there any coffee?"

"Just made a fresh pot." Henry turned and motioned for them to follow him to the kitchen.

After they all set down at the table with their coffee, Amanda said, "I guess this puts us out of the garden competition."

"Not a chance," Margaret disagreed. "As soon of the sheriff releases the backyard, it's back to work." She tapped her finger on the table.

"This competition is very important to you, isn't it?" Amanda was surprised at the determination written on her grandmother's face.

"Yes, well ..." Margaret picked at the edge of the placemat in front of her. "Your grandfather won the competition a few times when he was alive. He loved gardening and after he died ..." She sighed. "I kind of let the garden go, my heart just wasn't into it." Margaret looked up at Amanda, her blue eyes misty.

"I didn't know that." Amanda finally understood why it was so important for her grandmother to return the garden to its former glory. Reaching over to squeeze Margaret's hand, she declared, "We're going to win this competition."

"Thank you," Margaret whispered and smiled.

"How long do you think it will take for the sheriff to release the backyard?" Amanda asked, looking at Henry for answers. Since he was the former sheriff, he would have a general idea.

"Couple of days." He shrugged. "That's all I would think."

"Creepy, isn't it," Amanda said, as a shiver ran down her spine. "A body so close to the house."

Margaret nodded her head in agreement. "Who do you think did it?"

"Sheriff Thomas thinks it was a robbery gone bad." Henry shrugged one shoulder.

"But you don't?" Margaret asked, taking a sip of her coffee.

Henry answered, "Nope, I think if someone was going to break into the house, they would have waited for him to leave." Scratching his head, he continued. "If they were interrupted, there would have been glass or some other signs of a break in."

"Jonah said that Butch's wallet and watch were still on the body and he had a lot of cash on him," Amanda interjected.

"That settles it! Not a robbery," Margaret announced. "So someone followed him here and killed him."

"But who?" Henry questioned. "And why?"

"I could give you a few suspects," Amanda chimed in.

"Really?" Henry sounded intrigued.

"Marty Smith, for one," she continued, holding up one finger. "They were fighting outside the hardware store about Butch stealing jobs from him."

"Kind of flimsy motive." Margaret crinkled her nose.

"But people have killed for less," Henry suggested, leaning closer to hear more.

"Lydia Benson." Amanda held up two fingers. "She was dating Butch and he was two-timing her with Wendy," she continued. "She came to the diner to confront Wendy."

"Then Wendy should be a suspect, too," Margaret chimed in. "Same motive."

"She was at the diner with Amanda last night when he was killed," Henry reasoned, looking at Amanda to confirm his theory.

Shaking her head, she admitted, "No, she left to find Butch and confront him about what Lydia said. But I don't think she would kill anyone."

"We could ask her where she was," Henry suggested, picking at the edge of his placement.

"I did, today," Amanda answered. "She didn't find him and went home and ate some ice cream, then went to bed."

"By herself?" Henry asked, sounding doubtful.

"Yeah." Amanda sighed. "Not a very good alibi, huh."

"So we can't take her off the list of suspects." Henry gave her a sympathetic look.

"I guess not ... but I still don't think she did it." Amanda looked a little defeated. "Wendy mentioned a Ginger Meadows."

"The real estate agent?" Margaret's eyebrows shot up.

"I don't know. Never met her." Amanda shrugged. "She said Ginger and Butch were constantly fighting over child support."

"He wasn't paying?" Henry inquired.

"That and he wasn't even claiming the little boy as his," Amanda said, taking a sip of her coffee.

"That's enough to make a woman extremely mad," Margaret admitted, swiping at a long strand of silver hair that had fallen loose from her bun.

"So, crime of passion?" Henry suggested.

"Maybe. Anyway, I'm starving," Margaret announced, changing the subject. "Let's order pizza."

"Sounds great," Amanda agreed, as the doorbell rang. "I'll get it."

She hurried to the front door and opened it. Jonah was standing there with his hair a mess, looking tired. "Did you come to get Twinkie?"

"Yeah, sorry I'm so late," Jonah said, running his fingers through his hair.

"Not a problem. It's been a crazy day for everyone." Amanda motioned for him to come in the house. Twinkie came rushing down the stairs with a sneaker in his mouth.

"Give me that," she demanded, grabbing the shoe from his mouth. "I haven't taken him out for a while." Twinkie ran into the living room.

"That's okay, I can do it," Jonah offered.

"Have you eaten yet?"

"No," he said, shaking his head.

"Stay for dinner," Amanda suggested. "We ordered pizza."

"I don't want to impose." He looked a little

uncertain.

"You're not." Twinkie came back with his leash and laid it on the floor in front of Amanda and whined. "Someone needs to go out," she said, reaching down to hook the leash to his collar. "I'll take him. That's what you pay me for." She laughed.

"Mind if I come along with you?" he asked. "The fresh air will do me good."

"Come on, then." She motioned with her head for him to follow and yelled toward the kitchen. "Nana! Jonah's staying for pizza and we're taking Twinkie out, be back in a minute."

They walked down the steps and into the yard. Amanda stopped briefly, looking at the gate to the backyard and the yellow police tape warning people to stay away. Jonah eyed her cautiously before saying, "I'm sorry that your grandmother's garden plans are ruined."

Running her hand through her blonde hair she said, "She plans on continuing with the garden when the police are finished." Twinkie stopped to sniff a mailbox post. "How much longer do you think they will be?" Her blue eyes sparkled in the evening light.

"The police still haven't identified the murder weapon yet." He shrugged as they continued walking. "I suggested to Sheriff Thomas that maybe he take another look at the crime scene and look for something heavy and squared around the edges."

"You think the murder weapon is still here?" Amanda's eyes grew wide with shock.

"Maybe. It wouldn't hurt for them to look," he

said. They walked for a while in silence as Twinkie sniffed a lamp post. "Amanda, there's something I have to tell you." His expression was grave.

"That doesn't sound good." She looked at him expectantly.

"Don't be surprised if Sheriff Thomas questions Wendy about Butch's death," he mentioned carefully, aware that Amanda and Wendy were becoming good friends.

"That makes sense, they were dating," Amanda said, reaching down and rubbing Twinkie on the head.

He reached over and touched her shoulder. "There's more to it than that. I saw her fighting with him on Maple Street about 50 yards from the convenience store."

"What time was that?" Amanda asked, sounding surprised.

"About 6:45, I took Twinkie for a walk. Then, I went back home and fell asleep watching T.V.," he said, scratching his chin.

"That's strange. Wendy told me that she never saw Butch after she left the diner." Placing her hands on her hips, she continued, "Why do you think she lied?"

"Don't know. But it does make her look guilty," he stated.

"This is making my brain hurt," Amanda complained, rubbing her temples with both hands.

"Well, we don't have to talk about it anymore tonight," he suggested with a smile.

"Then you don't know my Nana and Henry."

She laughed, wagging her finger at him.

"Fine, how about we talk about something else for the rest of the walk back." He said.

"Sounds good," she agreed.

They talked about mundane things for a while before the street lamps started to light the sleepy streets of Juniper Falls. Jonah didn't like to see her in distress. Over the past few months he had grown very fond of Amanda Blakemore. He shoved his hands in the pockets of his blue jeans and kicked at a stray piece of gravel. "There's something— something I've been wanting to ask you?" This was the right time, he told himself.

She turned and looked up at him, her blue eyes sparkling in the lamp light. "Yes." Before he could open his mouth her cell phone started ringing.

"Hang on," she said, reaching into her pocket and pulling out her phone to answer it.

Watching her talk on the phone, Jonah debated with himself. Maybe this wasn't the right time. A lot had happened with the murder and the garden competition. Maybe he should wait, he told himself.

"That was Nana," she said, placing the phone back in her pocket. "Pizza's at the house." Turning to head back toward the house, she asked, "What did you want to say?"

"Nothing ..." Jonah shook his head, completely losing his nerve. "I'm starving. I can't wait to eat."

She gave him a confused look, then said, "Me, too!"

Chapter 6

Amanda awoke early the next morning, stretching her legs until her feet came into contact with a furry ball located at the foot of her bed. Wiggling her toes, she could hear a muffled, "Meow."

Peeking under the blankets, she asked, "How did you get under there?" Opening one yellow eye, Ghost gave her a very annoyed look. "You're not mad because I woke you up for a change." She laughed. She got out of bed and headed for the shower, glancing back at the bed to see the blankets bob up and down as Ghost repositioned himself. After taking a shower, Amanda blow dried her hair and wondered why Wendy would lie to her. Unless she had something to hide. Amanda heaved a deep sigh, feeling a little guilty suspecting her friend of murder. Amanda had learned over the last six months or so never judge a book by its cover.

Another thing about last night that kept bugging her was Jonah. She couldn't shake the feeling that her relationship with him was changing. Amanda wasn't sure how she felt about that. He was gorgeous, smart, funny, and kind. But she wasn't sure if she was ready for a relationship so soon after her divorce. "Oh, what are you worried about?" she asked her reflection in the mirror. "It's probably just your imagination." She made a face at herself before leaving to get some breakfast.

Ghost pounced off the bed to follow her, meowing his complaints the whole way.

Entering the kitchen, Amanda announced to the grouchy cat, "Nana's not up yet so breakfast is up to us. Tuna for you." She pointed at Ghost, who was sitting patiently tapping his tail on the floor. She opened a can of tuna, placing it in his bowl.

After starting the coffee, she opened the fridge and asked the large gray tomcat, "What should I have for breakfast?" The only response she received was the munching sounds of him eating the tuna. "You're no help," she complained. Looking over at the cat, she could see his gray tail twitch as he ate. She laughed, saying, "No, I don't think Nana would like tuna for breakfast." Turning back to the fridge, she exclaimed, "French Toast!"

By the time she got all the ingredients and mixed them together and placed the skillet on the stove, Margaret had walked into the kitchen.

"You're up and making breakfast," Margaret said, a surprised look on her face.

"Don't look so surprised. I've made breakfast before." Amanda laughed, pointing the spatula at her grandmother. "Although normally you wake up before me."

"I tossed and turned all night," Margaret informed Amanda. "Thinking about poor Butch."

"I know. It really creeps me out." Amanda set the plates on the table as Margaret took a seat. "Want some coffee?" Amanda asked. "Might help you wake up."

"Love some." Margaret smiled.

Amanda poured the coffee and put down the pot when Ghost started scratching at the back door. Without thinking, she pulled open the door and Ghost dashed out.

"I don't think we should let him out in the backyard since the police aren't finished yet," Margaret said, rubbing her eyes with the back of her hand.

"I forgot all about that." Amanda jerked the door open and called over her shoulder before running out after Ghost. "Watch the food."

The slender gray tomcat jumped off the bannister of the back porch. He ran to pounce on a butterfly he spotted perched on a flower down below, next to a large plastic garbage can. Amanda looked both ways to make sure no one was watching before running down the stairs, careful to turn wide and not step anywhere close to where the body was found.

Finally reaching the cat, she scooped him up fast before he could make a second attempt on the butterfly's life. He let out a loud meow in protest.

"You can't play out here yet," she said, rubbing under his chin to try to calm the grumpy cat. Turning back to the house, her eyes landed on bits and pieces of the old wooden gate that Henry had torn down. A shiver ran down her spine. The murder weapon—that was the first thought that popped into her mind.

"You could kill someone with a piece of that

old gate. Don't you think so, Ghost?" she mumbled, hugging the cat closer to her. "We need to tell Jonah." She hurried back around and into the house as quickly as her feet would carry her.

Amanda closed the door and set Ghost on the floor. Looking into her grandmother's blue eyes, she announced breathlessly, "I think I know what the murder weapon was."

Margaret blinked a few times, letting the words sink in. "It's … It's not still out there, is it?"

"What? No, or at least I don't think so." Shaking her head, Amanda continued. "Jonah said that Butch was hit with something heavy."

"Yeah," Margaret urged, taking a few steps closer to Amanda.

"The old metal gate that Henry took down!"

Amanda pointed over her shoulder toward the backyard.

"Some pieces did fall off when he tossed it into the trash." Margaret's eyes lit up with realization. "If that's true, the murder was spur of the moment."

"I have to tell Jonah," Amanda announced, just as the doorbell rang.

"Finish your breakfast, first." Margaret pointed at Amanda's plate. "I'll get that."

Amanda could hear Olive's voice floating from the other room.

As they entered the kitchen, Olive announced, "I know who the killer is!"

"Really!" Margaret and Amanda said in unison.

"Of course I do!" Olive smiled her cat-that-ate-the-canary smile. "I told you if I was as young as you, I could have been in the F.B.I." She nodded her head so her curly white hair with blue tint bounced with the motion.

"Oh, for heaven's sake, Olive! Spit it out," Margaret complained.

Looking a little put out by Margaret interrupting her shining moment, Olive blurted out, "Marty Smith."

"Really? You have proof?" Amanda asked, leaning forward in her chair and forgetting all about her breakfast.

"Proof? Of course, I have proof! I have a nose for these things." Olive patted the side of her nose with her index finger, her dramatics revived.

"So, what's your proof?" Margaret asked, trying to hurry Olive along.

"Marty and Butch were enemies." Olive patted her tight, blue-tinted curls before continuing. "They fought outside the hardware store the other day. Mabel Perkins saw them." She nodded, then holding up one crooked finger, she said, "Butch kept stealing Marty's lawn jobs."

"And?" Margaret asked.

"And—what?" Olive looked confused.

"That's all the evidence you got?" Margaret sounded exasperated. "Did you hear all that gossip while you were playing cards?"

Olive blinked innocently from behind her corrective lenses. "Yes, I did. But Mabel Perkins is a very reliable source."

"But not enough to convince me that Marty Smith killed anyone." Margaret announced, tossing her hands up in the air.

"I know he did it," Olive nearly screamed. "He's got those shifty eyes."

"Olive, without any hard evidence," Amanda tried to explain, "The sheriff can't make an arrest."

"Oh, my goodness," Olive interrupted Amanda. "Marty mows my lawn. If he knows that I know, he might kill me as well!" Olive started to panic.

"Olive, no one is going to kill you," Amanda said in a soothing voice. "Besides, he doesn't know that you know anything."

"Of course he knows," Olive looked shocked. "Everyone knows that I am the most enquiring person in all of Juniper Falls, and extremely intelligent, too!"

Margaret asked, "Do you think he's going to murder you in your sleep?"

"Maybe! This town has had quite the crime wave lately." Olive looked at Amanda for support. "What if he discovers that I told you two? You'll be in danger, too."

Amanda felt sorry for Olive, who looked genuinely scared. Turning toward Margaret, she said, "She does have a point about the increase in crime lately."

Margaret sighed and rubbed her temples as if she was getting a headache. "You can stay with us if it will make you feel better."

"Thanks, Margaret!" Olive smiled and grabbed Margaret's hand. "You're a true friend."

Amanda giggled and put her plate in the sink before saying, "I'm going over to talk to Jonah about my idea for the murder weapon."

Stepping outside, Amanda could feel the heat from the sun. It was still early and already the humidity was high today. It was going to be a scorcher. Looking over at Jonah's, she could see Marty's truck sitting in the driveway. Making her way over, she glanced around the side of the truck to see Marty standing on the porch talking to Jonah.

She took the opportunity to nose around the back of his truck. Nothing seemed to jump out at her, and it's not as though she thought she would find anything, but she couldn't resist.

Sighing, she stepped from behind the truck and called, "Hey guys!" Shielding her eyes from the sun, she continued, "It's going to be a hot one."

"Hey! Amanda, how are you?" Marty asked, giving her a big smile.

"Good, considering everything that's happened." She thought now would be as good of a time as any to get some information from him.

"Yeah," he said, scratching his chin. "Can't say that I'm sorry."

"Really?" Jonah chimed in. "You two didn't like each other?"

"No, we're business rivals." Marty shrugged one beefy shoulder. "Truth be told, didn't like him as a person much, either."

"He did have a very overwhelming personality," Amanda agreed, giving Marty an understanding smile. People always seemed to say more if they thought you agreed with them.

"Overwhelming is not the word I would use. Jerk is more like it," Marty informed her, looking down at his watch. "I better get to work now, since the grass isn't going to cut itself."

Jonah waited until Marty was out of earshot before saying, "No love lost between those two."

"Doesn't sound like it," Amanda agreed.

"They found Butch's truck abandoned down by the Falls," Jonah informed her quietly.

"That's kind of far from Nana's," she commented, placing her hands on her hips.

"Yeah, they're checking for fingerprints but I don't think they'll find any." He shrugged.

Hearing a loud bark and scratching coming from the door, Jonah said, "I think Twinkie wants to say hi." He walked into the house and motioned for Amanda to follow.

Twinkie danced around, wagging his tail, as Amanda reached down and rubbed his ears. "Hey, buddy." She kneeled down to talk to the massive St Bernard. "I've missed you." He licked her face. Apparently, he had missed her, too.

"I was just about to call you. Do you think you could take Twinkie for a little while?" Jonah asked, his brown eyes looking down at her. "Got some more tests to run for Sheriff Thomas."

"Sure thing." She hesitated before continuing. "Speaking of Sheriff Thomas—" she stood, shifting on her feet nervously. "You see, I kind of accidently let Ghost out in the backyard, but I ran out and grabbed him quickly."

"This is bad!" Jonah said, running his hand through his hair. "Did you touch anything?"

"No," she nearly shouted. "I grabbed Ghost and ran back inside."

"Good, you didn't disturb the crime scene." He let out a sigh of relief.

"But I do have good news." She smiled. "I think I know what the killer used to murder Butch."

"Really?" He sounded surprised.

"A piece of that old metal gate that Henry tore down."

Jonah looked at her for a long moment as if trying to absorb this new information. "You might be right. I'll have Sheriff Thomas send a deputy down to retrieve the old gate to see if it matches the wounds on Butch's body."

"That sounds great. Just don't tell him I went into the backyard." Her voice had a pleading tone.

"Your secret is safe with me." He gave her a bright smile.

"Great! I can take Twinkie now and you can come by later to pick him up."

Chapter 7

Amanda was out of breath. She stopped to take a deep breath then she grabbed the massive suitcase and started dragging it down the stairs of Olive's house. Twinkie stared at her, turning his head and giving her a confused look. "How many clothes does Olive need, anyways?" Amanda huffed, looking over at Twinkie. "Instead of just sitting there you could help." The massive dog licked her face and whined.

Finally making it to the bottom step, she plopped down on the floor next to him. "I know you would help if you could." She rubbed his head as she caught her breath.

Olive called from the living room, "Amanda, what's taking so long."

Amanda looked at Twinkie and whispered. "I don't think I'm going to survive this." She got up and walked into the bright yellow living room. "How many clothes do you need?"

"I just want to be prepared." Olive gave a shrug.

"For what," Amanda complained, pointing at the massive suitcase. "That thing is the size of Montana."

"That might be an exaggeration." Margaret

laughed. "But it is a lot of clothes. How long are you planning on staying?"

"Until he gets arrested." Olive stated.

"I was thinking about that," Margaret announced. "We need to rule out all the suspects on the list. That's why I took it upon myself to set up an appointment with Lydia Benson at Misty Waters Retirement Center. She's the admission director there, so she's going to give us a tour of the facility."

Amanda's mouth flew open. "What? Why?"

"That place is a death trap," Olive moaned.

"It is not! Besides, I'm not planning on living there. I just want to talk to Lydia and what better way." Margaret looked very pleased with herself. "She'll never suspect a thing."

"That's brilliant," Amanda said, amazed at her

grandmother's resourcefulness.

"Henry wants to come along, too," Margaret added.

"Count me out," Olive complained. "Once that place gets its hooks in you …" She wagged her finger in the air, then a motion outside the window caught her eye. Leaning forward in her chair, she peeped out the window. "Oh, no. He's here."

"Who's here?" Margaret questioned.

"Marty!" Olive's eyes looked like they were going to pop out of her head.

Amanda walked over and glanced out the window, "Olive! He's here to mow your lawn, not kill you." Olive didn't look convinced, so Amanda charged on. "Besides, we're here with you. He can't kill all of us."

"I think we should wait till he leaves," Olive whispered.

"Stop being ridiculous," Margaret announced, standing up from her chair and glancing out the window. "Besides, is he going to kill all of us and Mr. Peabody, who's sitting on his porch across the street?" Margaret sniffed. "Let's go."

"You mean, go outside with him?" Olive looked doubtful.

"That is where the car's located," Margaret pointed out.

"Don't worry, we have Twinkie with us," Amanda said and laughed. Everyone turned to look at the giant St Bernard sitting in the corner, scratching his brown ear with his hind leg.

"I feel so much safer," Olive announced

sarcastically.

Outside at the car, Amanda fought with the heavy suitcase to get it into the trunk. Twinkie was already in the back seat with his head hanging out the window, barking as if to encourage her with the battle. Marty waved from atop his riding mower he had just unloaded it from the trailer that he pulled behind his truck. Pulling up beside them, he climbed off his mower and said, "Let me get that for you."

"Thanks." Amanda said. Olive may not be happy to see him but she was.

"You going somewhere, Ms. Olive?" he asked, easily placing the suitcase inside the trunk and closing it.

"Staying with Margaret." She gave a forced

smile. "She's all torn up about this murder business."

"I could see why that would be upsetting," he said in return, giving Margaret a look of sympathy.

"She's afraid the killer might come back," Olive continued innocently. Amanda made a strangled noise as she tried to hold back her laughter, while Margaret rolled her eyes.

≈

The next day at Misty Waters Retirement Center, Amanda placed the car in park, then turned the key in the ignition and took a deep breath. Turning to her grandmother who was sitting in the passenger seat, Amanda said, "Tell me again. What's our story?"

Margaret grinned, unbuckling her seatbelt. "We're just here for information and for a tour of the facility."

"Won't they find this all a little strange?" Amanda questioned.

"No, people do this kind of thing all the time." Henry leaned forward from the backseat, patting her on the shoulder. "We're just planning ahead." He gave her a wink.

"If you say so," she said, opening the car door but still feeling unconvinced.

The trio made their way to the reception desk and a bubbly, red-haired woman escorted them into Lydia's office. The room was small with just enough space for a desk and chair, as well as two more chairs on the opposite side for potential clients. Amanda stood behind the two chairs, allowing Margaret and Henry to sit.

Amanda watched through the glass window that separated the small office from the hallway. She could see into another room where three elderly ladies in wheelchairs were chatting while assembling some kind of craft. They seemed happy, she thought.

"There she is," Margaret whispered, interrupting Amanda's thoughts.

Amanda could hear the clicking of Lydia's high heels on the marble floor. Lydia plastered a big smile on her face and extended her hand out toward Margaret. "Hello, Mrs. Blakemore, my name is Lydia Benson. I'm the admissions director here at Misty Waters Retirement Center."

"This is my granddaughter, Amanda, and neighbor, Henry Walters," Margaret introduced.

Lydia's smile slipped when her eyes landed on Amanda.

Amanda put on her most sincere smile and extended her hand. "Nice to see you again, Miss Benson."

Lydia looked a little rattled, but just for a moment, before recovering quickly. "You're here for a tour and some information about our lovely facility," she said, taking a seat behind the desk.

She reached into a drawer and produced some brochures. "Here you go." She handed Margaret and Henry each a brochure and started on a long-winded sales pitch that Amanda suspected Lydia could recite in her sleep. The only time Lydia stopped to take a breath was when the phone rang.

"Excuse me." Lydia reached over and picked

up the receiver. "Misty Waters Retirement Center. How may I assist you?" Amanda watched as Lydia grabbed a pen and opened up her appointment book and started writing. "Yes, Mr. Woodard, I can meet with you and your wife at 3:00 pm on Wednesday."

Amanda realized she needed to get a look at that appointment book. She slipped her purse off her shoulder and set it on the floor, pushing it under Margaret's chair with her foot.

Hanging up the phone, Lydia smiled an apology and said, "This is our busiest time of year. Shall we take that tour?"

≈

They completed the tour in about 20 minutes and were standing by the exit doors. "Thank you so much. This was very informative." Margaret shook

Lydia's hand.

"Oh ..." Amanda interrupted. "I forgot my purse in your office." Amanda turned to retrieve it when Henry stepped in front of Lydia and started asking questions to keep her there while Amanda ran back to get a look at the appointment book.

She entered the office, closed the door behind her, and pulled her phone out of her back pocket. Quickly she snapped some pictures of the last two weeks of appointments. Then Amanda grabbed her purse from under the chair and hurried down the hallway. When she saw Henry and Margaret, she called, "Found it." Amanda turned to Lydia and said, "I'm really sorry about Butch."

Lydia looked surprised and her eyes teared up as she choked out, "Thank you."

After exiting the building, Amanda hurried across the parking lot and climbed into the car when Henry asked, "Did you get a look at that appointment book?"

"Better than that." She beamed. "I took pictures."

"That's my girl." Henry leaned forward and patted Amanda's shoulder.

"I think that was the most boring twenty minutes of my life," Amanda complained, as she started the car.

"At least you didn't have to pretend to be interested and ask questions." Margaret laughed, shaking her head.

"Thank heaven for that." Amanda laughed, pulling out of the parking lot.

Amanda rushed into the house and started printing off the pictures before changing into her work clothes, which consisted of a red T-shirt that said "Deb's Diner" in small print over her heart and a pair of comfortable blue jeans. Grabbing the pictures off the printer, she stopped at the top of the stairs. She could hear a man's voice filtering its way through the air.

"Jonah," she whispered, her stomach doing a little flutter at the thought of him. Amanda had been thinking a lot about him lately. A smile touched her lips as she continued on the path to the living room. When she entered the room, she saw Jonah and Twinkie talking to Henry.

"Hey, guys," Amanda said, to let her presence be known.

Jonah's face lit up with a bright smile. "Hey." His eyes took in her shirt and a look of disappointment flicked across his handsome features before he could hide it. "You going to work?"

"Yeah, Deb asked if I could go in a little early today." She shrugged and continued, "I thought I might as well, since the garden is off limits." Amanda handed Henry the photos before bending down and rubbing Twinkie's ears. His tail thumped on the hardwood floor and his tongue was hanging out the side of his mouth.

"Well, I come bearing good news," Jonah announced. "Sheriff Thomas has released your backyard."

"That's great," Amanda exclaimed.

"This calls for a celebration." Henry clapped Jonah on the back.

"I'll get us some drinks," Margaret suggested, then disappeared into the kitchen.

"I wish I could stay." Amanda sounded sad. "But I've got to go to work." Looking around, she asked, "Where's Olive?"

Setting down a tray filled with coffee and chocolate cake on the coffee table, Margaret waved her hand and answered, "She left a note saying she would be back later, and not to worry."

"That's strange," Amanda said, a bad feeling starting to form in the pit of her stomach.

"Everything about that woman is strange," Henry grumbled.

"Life would be boring without her and you

know it, Henry Walters," Margaret scolded, as she handed him a cup of coffee.

"That's my cue to leave." Amanda laughed and walked out the door.

Chapter 8

Amanda tossed her keys into her purse as she entered the diner and her mouth fell open in shock. Wendy was there, waiting tables. Amanda wanted to talk to Wendy about lying, but she had never imagined she would be here. Out of the corner of her eye, Amanda saw Deb waving her arms frantically from the small window that separated the dining area from the kitchen, trying to get Amanda's attention.

Darting into the kitchen, Amanda whispered, "What's going on? Why is Wendy here?" Amanda hung up her purse in the cabinet and grabbed a clean apron off the wooden peg on the wall.

"The poor thing came in this morning, said she needed to work to keep her mind off of Butch." Deb shook her head before turning back to the stove to stir a massive pot of chicken and dumplings.

"Maybe I should talk to her?" Amanda offered, glancing through the window at Wendy, who looked pale and miserable.

"Hopefully you'll get farther then me," Deb whispered, wiping her hands on her apron. "Poor thing, she's devastated ... just devastated."

Amanda sighed. "I'll wait till the rush is over."

"Give her some pie, it always makes me feel better." Deb smiled, pointing at the freshly baked apple pies sitting on the cooling rack.

Hearing the sound of the bell over the door, Amanda went out to see who had come in. Cassie Hardy climbed on a stool at the end of the counter and smiled brightly at Amanda. Her chestnut hair was pulled back into a ponytail.

"Hey, stranger," Amanda called to her friend. "Long time no see."

"I'm sorry, I've been so busy at the animal clinic," Cassie apologized, giving Amanda a heartfelt smile. "We'll have dinner together soon—and I'll pay!"

"Dinner, how can I refuse? You're forgiven." Amanda laughed. "What can I get for you?" She grabbed her order pad and pen out of her apron pocket.

"Just give me the special. To go, please,"

Cassie answered.

"One special, coming up." Amanda jotted it all down then placed the order with Deb.

The jingle of the bell announced another customer. Amanda turned to see Jacob taking a seat in his usual spot.

"Hello, Jacob." She made her way over to him, "How are you, today?"

"I'm fine." He smiled. "How's your grandmother's garden coming along?"

Amanda glanced over at Wendy before answering, making sure she was out of earshot. "We had a small setback, but hopefully we'll be back on track by tomorrow."

"Good. The more contestants, the better. Just don't forget to turn in your entry form," he reminded

Amanda.

"I won't," she reassured him, taking out her order pad. "What can I get for you?"

"A pulled pork sandwich, fries, and some sweet tea." He gave her a big smile.

Amanda gave him a surprised look. "Something new today?"

"I thought that it's time for a change." He winked.

"Nothing wrong with that." She returned his smile.

≈

The evening went along rather smoothly. When all the customers had left, Amanda decided this was the best time to approach Wendy about lying. "Wendy, do you want some pie?" Amanda offered in an attempt to break the ice.

"Sure," Wendy answered, climbing onto a stool at the corner.

Amanda placed a piece of pie on a saucer and handed it to Wendy. "I need to talk to you about something," she started gravely.

"I know what you're going to say," Wendy interrupted, as she rubbed her hand over her face. "But working helps keep my mind off of things."

"That's not what I was going to say." Amanda had a serious expression on her face. She didn't really know how to approach the subject so she just blurted it out. "You lied to me about seeing Butch after you left here. Jonah told me that he saw you arguing with Butch the night he was killed."

Wendy burst into tears. "I'm sorry ... I was

just so embarrassed." She swiped at the tears running down her face.

Amanda sit on the stool next to Wendy and gave her a quick hug. Deb set coffee down on the counter. Then she, too, gave Wendy a reassuring hug. "Oh, you poor thing, tell us what happened."

"I found Butch at the convenience store and when I asked him about Lydia, he acted like it was no big deal. The more upset I got, the more he laughed. So I slapped him and went straight home." She turned to Amanda and grabbed her hand, pleading, "You have to believe me."

By the frightened look on Wendy's face, Amanda was inclined to believe her story—or at least to believe she was scared about something. "I believe you," Amanda said, patting Wendy's hand.

"But don't be surprised if the sheriff questions you."

"Surely he won't think Wendy's capable of murder?" Deb asked, concerned.

"Let's hope not, but you never know," Amanda said.

≈

Amanda was searching through her purse, looking for her keys as she made her way to her car. Her feet were killing her after waiting tables for hours. Headlights flashed from a large pickup truck whizzing past as she pulled her keys out, trying to unlock the door. Then another set of headlights flashed and Olive called from her blue sedan, "Hurry up!" She was waving her arm frantically. "Get in!"

"What? Oh, no! Did something happen to Nana?" Amanda asked, rushing toward the car.

"Hurry!" Olive nearly screamed.

Amanda jumped into Olive's car, panic gripping her chest. "What happened? Is Nana okay?" she choked out, as Olive squealed the tires taking off. Amanda fumbled with her seatbelt as Olive turned the corner a little too fast, making Amanda brace herself on the door with her hand to keep from sliding into it. "Olive, this isn't the way to the hospital," Amanda announced, with panic in her voice.

"We're not going to the hospital." Olive turned down another street.

"What's going on?" Amanda nearly screamed.

"We're following Marty Smith." Olive said, glancing over to look at Amanda.

"Marty Smith!" Amanda's eyes nearly popped

out of her head. "Are you saying that nothing happened to Nana?"

"Not that I know of. I haven't seen her since lunchtime." Olive gave Amanda an innocent look.

"You nearly gave me a heart attack!" Amanda complained, placing her hand over her heart as if to help calm herself. "Why are we following Marty?"

Olive looked at Amanda like she had just grown another head. "He's guilty." Olive tossed her thumb back at herself. "And I'm going to catch him."

"So, you're stalking him," Amanda stated. "There's laws against that."

"We're not stalking ... We're observing." Olive smiled. "Totally different."

"And I'm going along for the ride." Amanda sighed, pulling out her phone and sending a text to

Nana telling her that she would be late and that Olive was with her. She told Nana not to worry, she would explain later. They turned down another side street keeping a respectable distance so Marty wouldn't notice them. Surprisingly, Olive was really good at this, Amanda thought. "Where exactly are we?"

"Oak Lane. It's on the edge of town," Olive answered, leaning forward to see over the steering wheel.

"Oh, he's pulling over." Amanda pointed, watching Marty's massive pickup truck park on the street in front of a white bungalow. Olive quickly pulled her blue sedan into the driveway of a vacant house across the street and a few doors down that had a "for sale" sign in the front yard. They had a good view from this spot. Olive quickly turned off her lights and motor. "Grab my binoculars out of the glove box," she told Amanda. Olive unbuckled her seat belt.

Retrieving the binoculars, Amanda held them up. "Really?"

Olive shrugged one shoulder. "What? I use them for bird watching."

"Uh, huh." Amanda wasn't convinced. "Since we're already here," she sighed, unbuckling her seatbelt, too. Then both she and Wendy turned around and kneeled in their seats so they could peer out the back glass.

Olive complained, "I can't see him."

"Here." Amanda handed Olive the binoculars. "He's getting out of his truck."

They watched as Marty climbed out of his truck and started up the sidewalk. Amanda turned her head and said, "You know this is probably his house."

"Pay dirt," Olive announced, not bothering to listen to anything Amanda said.

"What?" Amanda quickly turned her head to see Marty locked in a lover's embrace with a blonde woman but she couldn't see the woman's face. "Who is that?" Amanda asked, trying to lean closer to get a better look.

"That's Ginger Meadows." Olive nodded her head. "Butch's old girlfriend and the mother of his child."

Amanda's mouth fell open. "So not only was Butch stealing Marty's jobs, but he was also mistreating the woman Marty loves."

"The plot thickens," Olive cackled, wagging her eyebrows.

"I have to admit you may be on to something," Amanda told Olive.

"I told you, if I was your age I could be in the FBI," Olive announced, turning back to her binoculars.

They watched as Marty and Ginger made their way into the house. "I guess we can go home," Amanda said, turning back around in her seat.

"What? Why?" Olive sounded confused.

"There's nothing more to see," Amanda said, to counter act Olive's confusion.

"With these I can see inside the house," Olive said, waving the binoculars at Amanda. "They're perfect for that kind of thing."

"We are not staying to watch the windows steam up," Amanda exclaimed, and then continued pointing her finger at Olive's binoculars. "And I don't even want to know how you found out those were perfect for looking through windows."

"Fine," Olive huffed, starting the car.

≈

When Olive and Amanda returned home, they found Margaret and Henry still up sitting in the living room looking through the pictures Amanda had taken of Lydia's appointment book.

"I was right! I was right," Olive told them, as she plopped down on the couch beside Margaret.

Margaret looked from Olive to Amanda with a confused expression on her face. "Right about what?"

"Marty Smith." Olive smiled as she adjusted her glasses.

Margaret's mouth fell open in shock and she glanced at Henry, who wore the same expression on his face. "He's the killer!" Margaret said stunned.

"That's right." Olive nodded her head with a smile pasted on her face.

"We don't know that for sure," Amanda interrupted, putting her hand on Olive's shoulder. "But we did see him and Ginger Meadows all hot and heavy earlier."

"The real estate agent? The one with the baby who belongs to Butch?" Margaret inquired.

"It sure is looking pretty bad for him," Henry chimed in.

"I told you. My killer radar has never failed me yet." Olive slapped her knee and smiled at her own wit. They all looked at her as if she had completely lost her mind.

"I never knew you were afflicted with such a thing, Olive," Henry said, muffling a chuckle.

"Absolutely, it's kind of like women's intuition but stronger," Olive stated, as serious as a heart attack. Amanda struggled not to laugh at the serious look written on Olive's face.

"Well, I wouldn't know anything about women's intuition," Henry said, laughing and shaking his head.

"No I suppose you wouldn't," Olive agreed, looking off into space as if contemplating his answer.

"The one thing we do know is that it's not

Lydia Benson," Margaret interrupted.

"We do?" Amanda asked. "How?"

"Yes, we do," Henry agreed. "According to her appointment book, she was in a meeting with Everett Watt's grandson, Lucas."

"Henry confirmed it by calling Lucas about an hour ago. Lucas said he was with Lydia until after nine o'clock," Margaret chimed in.

"She didn't have enough time to drive from the retirement center to here and kill Butch," Henry said.

"Of course it's not her. It's Marty," Olive nearly yelled. "I don't know why I bother." She got up from her seat and huffed. "I'm going to bed."

Chapter 9

The backyard had an eerie feel to it, Amanda

thought, as a shiver ran down her spine. Even

though they had removed the body, along with all

signs that a murder had taken place here, it still had

a creepy vibe. Maybe it was because she was all

alone in the backyard. Well, not completely alone.

Ghost was lounging on the bannister, enjoying the

morning sun. Nana and Olive had gone to pick up

more flowers, while Henry must be running a little

late. Taking a deep breath, she placed her hands on her hips. "Stop being a baby," she scolded herself.

She decided the fence wasn't going to paint itself so she sorted through the painting supplies and grabbed a brush and gallon of stain Amanda was acutely aware of every sound as she worked to get the can of paint opened, then poured it into a plastic container with a handle.

Dipping the brush into the white paint, she had just started making long strokes when the gentle clack of the gate closing behind her drew her attention. "Jonah." To her dismay, her voice sounded a little too relieved by his presence. She hoped her nervousness wasn't as obvious to him.

"Hey, neighbor," he called with a wave of his hand. Twinkie followed close behind, sniffing everything. "Looks like you started without me."

If he noticed her nervousness, he didn't let it show.

"I didn't know if you were going to make it," she answered, making another swipe with the paint brush. "You know, because of the murder investigation."

"My part is pretty well done. It's all up to the sheriff now." He smiled, giving her a salute. "So, I'm reporting for duty."

"Grab a brush from over there." She pointed to a small patio table that had been converted into a work station.

He returned with a brush and dipped it into the paint can, before asking, "Where is everybody?"

"Flower run." She glanced over at him. Jonah

looked good in his jean shorts and dark blue T-shirt. "So, do they have any suspects?"

"The only thing I know is they were going to question Wendy today." He gave her a nervous glance but continued painting.

"That doesn't surprise me. She did have an argument with him right before he died." Amanda shrugged. "She told me about it last night."

"She did?" He looked surprised.

"Yeah, I told her that you saw them." Amanda informed him. "You don't mind, do you?"

"No, she would have found out from the sheriff, anyways," he answered. "Besides, I don't think Wendy killed anyone. It would take someone pretty strong to kill a man Butch's size."

"Let's hope the sheriff comes to the same

conclusion."

≈

After a long hot bath, Amanda sat on the couch in her pink fluffy robe with Ghost on her lap. The hot water had soothed her sore muscles and was helping her to relax. Laying her head back with her eyes closed, she mindlessly stroked Ghost's soft fur. He was purring and gently tapping his tail to a tune only he could hear.

Olive came in and plopped down on the couch beside Amanda, causing the large tomcat to let out a protesting "Meow."

Olive looked at Ghost and huffed, "That's the grumpiest cat I have ever seen."

Amanda scratched Ghost under the chin and said defensively, "He's not grumpy."

"Girls," Margaret interjected, as she came into the living room carrying the newspaper. "I was thinking we need to go house shopping."

Olive and Amanda looked at her as if she had just grown another head. "What!"

"You don't want to sell your house just because you had a dead guy in the backyard," Olive wailed. "Besides, no one will want to buy it now, anyways." Olive gave her friend a dismissive wave of her hand.

"No," Margaret interrupted, before Olive could go off on some long-winded speech about the housing market in Juniper Falls not being what it used to. "This is why." Margaret held up the newspaper and pointed at a picture of Ginger Meadows.

Amanda leaned forward to the dismay of Ghost, who was still perched on her lap. "I think that's a brilliant plan."

"I don't understand ... unless you think that Marty and Ginger were in it together." Olive perked up at the thought of proving herself right. "It *is* possible that they were in it together." Giving them a determined look, she added, "A good detective must go where the clues take her, so count me in."

"There's only one way to find out." Margaret smiled and tilted her head to one side. "She's having an open house on Maple Street tomorrow."

"This is so exciting!" Olive exclaimed, giddily rubbing her hands together.

≈

After arriving at the open house the next day,

Amanda thought the house looked very quaint. It was a little red cottage with white trim and beautiful flowers planted in front of the wrap-around porch. They stepped in through the solid oak door into the living room. The room had hardwood floors and deep green walls with a small table placed in the center of the room. Atop the table were brochures with information about the house and the real estate company.

Ginger called from upstairs, "Be right with you. Help yourself to coffee and donuts located in the kitchen." The donuts were arranged in an inviting manner on a tray sitting on the marble countertop.

Olive reached over to pick up a cream-filled donut with pink sprinkles on top. Amanda couldn't help herself. She leaned in close to Olive just as she was about to take a bite and whispered, "I wouldn't, what if they're poisoned?" Amanda topped it off with a serious look.

Olive's arm was frozen in mid-air and her mouth was hanging open. She looked at the donut as if it were a snake about to strike. Amanda giggled and snatched a glazed donut off the tray and took a big bite, then smiled.

"Not funny," Olive grumbled, not looking the least bit amused, before taking a bite of her donut.

"I wish Henry could have come," Amanda mused, taking a cup of coffee from Margaret.

"He's too busy laying the patio stones," Margaret commented, handing Olive a cup. "I'm so glad Pastor Max offered to help."

"Me too," Olive chimed in. "Jonah and Henry need all the help they can get."

Ginger entered the kitchen dressed in a dark blue business suit and heels. Her mousy brown hair was pulled up in a French twist and she had a smile plastered on her face. "Hello, Ms. Olive and Ms. Margaret, it's nice to see you again."

"Good morning." Margaret gestured toward Amanda and continued, "This is my granddaughter, Amanda."

Amanda stepped forward and shook Ginger's hand. "Nice to meet you."

"So, are you the one looking for a house?" Ginger asked politely. "Or are you planning on relocating, Ms. Margaret?"

That was Margaret's cue to start fishing for

information. "I'm not ...well—" She let out a dramatic sigh. "You did hear about what happened ... in my backyard?"

Ginger had a strange look on her face before answering, "Yes."

"It was awful," Olive chimed in dramatically. "Makes one wonder what's happening to our little town." She shoved the remainder of her donut in her mouth.

"Did you know Butch?" Margaret asked innocently.

"We dated a long time ago," Ginger answered quickly, glancing around, trying to look for an escape.

"She knows him," Olive announced, nudging Margaret in the side with her elbow before returning her attention to Ginger. "Your mother is so proud of that little boy of yours." Smiling an innocent old lady smile, Olive continued. "Isn't Butch Henderson your little boy's daddy?"

"Yes, he is, but—" Ginger looked completely uncomfortable, shifting her weight from one foot to another. "Truthfully, I haven't seen Butch in a long time. My lawyer does most of the communication between us."

"That's so sad," Olive said sympathetically. "Is he one of those dead-beat dads?" She gave Ginger a pitying look.

"Guys like that make me so mad," Amanda said, joining in the conversation.

"It's my own fault," Ginger complained. "I should have known. The whole time we dated, he cheated on me."

"My ex-husband cheated on me. The big jerk," Amanda informed. "My divorce was just finalized."

"She didn't even tell off that floozy who stole her husband," Olive complained, giving Amanda a sour look.

"Good riddance to bad rubbish is what I say," Margaret announced with a nod of her head.

"Some men are just dogs." Ginger shook her head. "Butch even had another girl pregnant the same time I was."

"He probably denies her baby, too," Olive huffed in disgust.

"He probably would have, but she killed herself before ..." Ginger let her voice trail off.

"That's terrible," Margaret gasped.

"That's why Butch moved away. He felt like people blamed him." Ginger gave a little shrug of her shoulders. "Truthfully, I was surprised when he came back."

Voices floated in from the living room and interrupted their conversation. Ginger straightened her posture and gave her suit jacket a little tug. "You ladies look around and just give a yell if you have any questions," Ginger said, before walking away to greet a couple who had come to see the house.

Chapter 10

"The patio looks beautiful," Margaret exclaimed. The dark gray stone was surrounded by fresh sod and outlined by brightly colored flowers. "I can't wait for the new patio furniture," she added. The others quickly agreed before resuming their tasks to put the finishing touches on the project.

Amanda was spreading mulch around the various new shrubs and flowers when Pastor Max came up behind her, carrying another bag of mulch.

"Thanks, I'm out," she said, as she emptied the remains of her bag into the flower bed. "Can I ask you a question?" she asked before he could walk away.

"Sure." He gave her a big smile. They had become friends since she had arrived in Juniper Falls.

"This is going to sound a little morbid," she said. He gave her a questioning glance after that statement, but she pushed on. "So, do you remember doing a funeral for a young girl who committed suicide in the last few years?"

"Hmmm." He tilted his head to the side in thought. "Not that I can recall."

"Oh." She sounded a little disappointed.

"Can I ask you why you want to know?" He swiped at the sweat on his forehead with his gloved hand.

"Well, it's something Ginger Meadows said about Butch." She gave him a sideways glance.

"Are you looking into his murder?" Pastor Max questioned quietly.

"Sort of, Olive is all stirred up about it … and it did happen in our backyard." Amanda sounded like she was trying to convince him.

"I'm not judging." He held up his hands in the air. "Just let me give you a piece of advice. Don't get into anything too dangerous. I would hate to have to do your funeral."

"I would hate that, too." She said laughing. "I promise I'll try to stay safe."

"You could try one of the other churches in town. Just because I didn't perform the service doesn't mean someone else didn't."

She perked up. "I didn't think of that."

He started to walk away, then turned to say, "I do remember a girl a few years back who committed suicide. I didn't officiate over her funeral." He rubbed his chin. "I think her name was Linda something." Max sighed. "So sad."

"Thanks, I'll ask Olive later. Maybe the name will ring a bell," Amanda commented.

≈

Henry carried a glass of lemonade over to Jonah, who was spreading mulch on the other side of the yard. "Time for a small break," Henry announced, handing the glass to Jonah.

"Sounds like an excellent idea," Jonah said, taking a long drink from the glass. They stood in silence for a few minutes looking over the backyard.

"I think you might have a little competition." Henry nodded his head toward Amanda and Pastor Max. Jonah's eyes scanned the scene until they landed on Amanda laughing at something Pastor Max said. Jonah felt a stab of jealously.

"I wouldn't wait too long. You might miss your chance," Henry said, then squeezed the younger man's shoulder and walked away. Jonah watched Henry in disbelief. Was he that transparent in his feelings for Amanda, he asked himself.

≈

"Amanda, could you do a favor for me?" Margaret called from the patio, laying the phone down on the table.

"Sure," Amanda answered, walking toward

her grandmother.

"Could you take the entry form over to Jacob Marsdale's?" She handed Amanda the paperwork. "I just got off the phone with him. He said not to ring the doorbell. He'll be in the backyard."

Twinkie barked and danced around when he heard the word backyard, making Amanda laugh. "You can come, too."

Chapter 11

Amanda and Twinkie walked the three blocks
it took to get to Jacob's house. His ranch-style home
was neatly kept. All the bushes were expertly
trimmed, while the flower beds were perfectly
arranged. They made their way around the side of
the house into the backyard.

"Hello," called Amanda, when the middle-
aged man came into view. Twinkie danced with
excitement at all the new smells. Amanda reached

down and released the massive dog from his leash. He darted around, smelling everything in sight throughout the fenced-in backyard.

"Amanda, it's so nice to see you again," Jacob said jovially, pulling off his gloves.

"Your garden is beautiful." She smiled, motioning to his backyard.

"Thank you." Jacob smiled with pride. "I love gardening."

"It shows," she assured him, reaching into her pocket and pulling out some papers. "Here is the entry form for the garden competition."

"Excellent, let me run these inside." He took the forms and asked, "Would you like some lemonade?"

"Sure." Amanda smiled, watching as he

climbed the three steps to reach the backdoor before disappearing into the house.

Hearing a loud snort, Amanda turned to see Twinkie tossing dirt as fast as his giant paws could move. "Twinkie ... No," she yelled, running as fast as she could and trying to pull the massive dog away by his collar. "You are in big trouble, mister!"

She tugged at his collar as hard as she could and finally got Twinkie to reluctantly move away from the hole. Looking down at the damage, a piece of plastic caught her eye. Reaching down, she brushed away some of the dirt from the clear plastic that was wrapped around a bloody piece of wood.

"That's too bad." Jacobs's voice made Amanda jump. "I really liked you ..." He shook his head and pushed his wire-framed glasses back up the bridge of his nose with his index finger. "Now I'm going to have to kill you," he announced, without any feeling in his voice as he reached for the shovel.

"You ... you killed Butch." Amanda's voice shook with fear as she slowly started backing away. "But ... Why?"

"He took everything from me." Jacob kept his voice calm so not to alarm Twinkie.

"I don't understand?" She was trying to buy time. She glared around for anything she could use as a weapon.

"My daughter, Linda, killed herself because of him." His voice started to raise as his hand tightened around the handle of the shovel, betraying his anger. Twinkie's ears perked up and he started to growl.

"I understand that you're angry," Amanda

pleaded, raising her hand and grabbing Twinkie by the collar with the other. She was afraid that Jacob could hurt Twinkie with that shovel.

"Do you," he yelled. "My wife left me because of what HE did," he complained, taking a step toward Amanda.

Amanda's blue eyes caught movement as Jonah entered the backyard. Quickly, before Jonah could make his presence known, Amanda blurted out, "I completely understand why you killed Butch, but killing me will only make things worse."

Jonah froze at her last words, realizing the gravity of the situation. He crept up slowly toward Jacob.

"I've come this far..." Jacob shrugged his shoulders.

At those words, Jonah rushed Jacob from behind, knocking both men off balance and causing them to hit the ground hard. Twinkie jerked, trying to break free from Amanda's tight grasp. The St. Bernard started growling and barking at the two men wrestling in the dirt. Amanda kicked the shovel out of reach, still holding onto Twinkie's collar.

The struggle lasted only a few minutes before Jacob gave up, being outmatched by the younger man. Jonah held him on the ground as Amanda called the police.

≈

Standing beside one of the Juniper Falls black and white police cars, Amanda and Jonah watched as Sheriff Thomas shoved Jacob into the backseat. "Wow, who would have thought ..." Jonah said.

"Definitely not Olive. She's going to be so disappointed it wasn't Marty." Amanda gave a small laugh. "Why did you come anyway? Not that I'm complaining," she quickly added.

"I ..." Jonah's face turned red as he looked down at Twinkie, who was dancing and whining, wanting to be turned loose so he could be part of the commotion. "I wanted to ask you if you would be my date for the garden party."

"Oh." Amanda's blue eyes grew wide as her stomach did a flip of excitement.

At her silence, he rushed, "Unless someone else has already asked." He kicked at a piece of gravel.

"No," she blurted out. "I mean, no one else has asked." She smiled shyly. "I would love to be your date for the garden party."

A deputy interrupted, saying, "Miss Blakemore, the sheriff wants to ask you a few more questions."

≈

Amanda ran her hands down the sides of her dress as she looked at herself in the mirror. Her stomach was fluttering with excitement. Ghost rubbed against her ankles when the doorbell rang. Amanda quickly patted her blonde hair, which she had neatly arranged in a sweeping up-do. "Here we go," she whispered to the cat, and quickly opened the door. "Hello." She smiled at Jonah. He looked handsome in his dark blue suit and neatly cropped hair.

"Good evening," he said, handing her a

bouquet of pink roses. "These are for you." He flashed her a brilliant smile.

"They are so beautiful." She took the flowers from him and deeply breathed in their alluring scent.

"You look beautiful," Jonah announced.

"You don't look too bad yourself." She chuckled. "And the same goes for you, too, Twinkie. Is that a new collar?" He was wearing a red collar with a bow tie on it.

"Yes, and he's very proud of it," Jonah whispered with a playful smile.

"Let me put these in some water and we can join everyone else at the party," she said.

"I'll wait here, then," he announced. Amanda gave him a strange look.

He laughed at her expression. "I wouldn't

want people to talk. Who knows what could happen, if I go in there alone with you?" He shrugged. "You may take advantage of me."

She rolled her eyes and said, "I'll try to control myself, but if you're scared…" She disappeared into the house.

Returning quickly, she closed the door behind her. "Are you two fellas ready for our big entrance?" Amanda asked.

"I think Twinkie might outshine both of us with that new collar," Jonah joked, offering his arm to Amanda.

"He does look quite dashing." She giggled, looping her arm in his. "I think I can endure it if you can."

They entered the garden through the new

wooden gate that Henry and Jonah had installed. The backyard garden was lit up with tiny Fairy lights and there were candles placed on the small tables located in small sitting areas throughout the garden. A long table had been set up for food and drinks, along with a giant trophy that was displayed in the center.

Amanda and Jonah chatted their way through the crowd of party-goers to where Margaret, Henry, and Olive were standing. "I hear congratulations are in order," Jonah announced jovially, as he shook Margaret's hand. "First place in the garden competition gives you definite bragging rights." He laughed.

"I couldn't have done it without all of you." She beamed.

Olive elbowed her way closer to Jonah and interjected, "And with all that prize money, the church can finally get a new roof." She batted her eyes at Jonah through her purple-rimmed spectacles.

"Miss Olive, don't you look beautiful tonight." His flattery caused her face to flush from the compliment.

"I was beginning to think we wouldn't finish in time," Henry said, handing Amanda and Jonah each a glass of punch.

"Who would have, thought that Jacob was a killer?" Margaret announced shaking her head.

"Not me!" Olive declared. "I would have laid money that Marty was the killer." She placed her hand across her chest in a dramatic gesture.

"It's so sad about his daughter killing herself."

Margaret sighed.

"Don't be a party pooper, Margaret," Olive scolded. "You two go and enjoy yourselves." She wagged her eyebrows at them. "No use hanging out with us old folks."

≈

The next few hours flew by so quickly and before they knew it the party started to break up. Jonah asked Amanda to dance one last time. A slow song was playing as they moved across the dance floor. She could smell the aroma of his cologne and feel the closeness of his body to hers. The song came to an end a far too quickly, leaving Amanda a little sad.

"I guess it's time to call it a night," he said quietly, then hesitated for a moment, not letting go of her hand.

"I'll walk you," Amanda offered, following close behind him.

They gathered up Twinkie and strolled out the gate onto the sidewalk that was lit by the street lamp.

"I had a really good time with you tonight." She smiled up at him.

"Me too." He leaned in closely as a cool breeze swirled around them. Jonah reached up gently, tilting up her face, making her eyes sparkle in the lamplight. Softly he pressed his lips to hers. Amanda leaned into him as their kiss became more demanding. The world around them seemed to disappear. Jonah finally broke away and just stared intently into her eyes.

Twinkie made a loud whine and rolled onto his back and started wiggling, making loud grumbling noises. "I think I better get him home." Jonah laughed. "It's way past his bedtime."

Amanda turned to walk away and Jonah grabbed her by the wrist and pulled her close. Quickly, he brushed a kiss onto her lips. Her blue eyes widened in surprise. Jonah nodded his head toward her grandmother's house. Amanda glanced at the house just in time to see the curtains flutter, as if someone was just peering from the window.

"That should get them talking." He gave her a wink and she giggled in response.

THe ENd

Author Information

I hope that you enjoyed the book!

I am an independent author and do it all on my own.

So if you liked the book please feel free to leave a

review.

If you're interested in future books follow me on

Facebook at Amy Phipps Author

Books Currently Available

A Bazaar Murder

Board to Death

Made in the USA
Lexington, KY
09 April 2017